The Three Little Pigs

Stories adapted by Shirley Jackson
Illustrated by Giles Hargreaves
Series designed by Jeannette Slater

Copyright © 1999 Egmont World Limited.
All rights reserved.
Published in Great Britain by Egmont World Limited,
Deanway Technology Centre, Wilmslow Road,
Handforth, Cheshire SK9 3FB
Printed in Germany
ISBN 0 7498 4358 6

pigs

wolf

straw

 hair

wood

 chin

bricks

Once upon a time,
the three little pigs
left home.

w words   **three   left   home**

"I will build a house of straw," said the first little pig.

And he did.

words **build house of first And he did**

The wolf came.

"Little pig, little pig,
let me come in," said
the wolf.

w words **came let come in**

"Not by the hair on my chinny chin chin!" said the first little pig.

"I will huff and I will puff and I will blow your house down," said the wolf.

And he did. The house of straw fell down.

words **huff puff blow your down fell**

"I will build a house of wood," said the second little pig.

And he did.

words **second**

The wolf came.

"Little pig, little pig,
let me come in," said
the wolf.

new words

"Not by the hair on my chinny chin chin!" said the second little pig.

new words

"I will huff and I will puff and I will blow your house down," said the wolf.

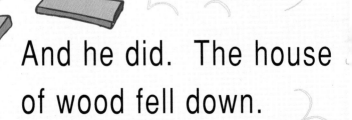

And he did. The house of wood fell down.

"I will build a house of bricks," said the third little pig.

And he did.

w word **third**

The wolf came.

"Little pig, little pig,
let me come in," said
the wolf.

"Not by the hair on
my chinny chin chin!"
said the third little pig.

new words

"I will huff and I will puff and I will blow your house down," said the wolf.

new words

The wolf huffed and he puffed.

The wolf fell down!